BY ROBERTO CALASSO

# THE TABLET OF DESTINIES

# THE TABLET OF DESTINIES

# ROBERTO CALASSO

TRANSLATED FROM THE ITALIAN
BY TIM PARKS

FARRAR, STRAUS AND GIROUX

NEW YORK

Farrar, Straus and Giroux
120 Broadway, New York 10271

Library of Congress Cataloging-in-Publication Data
Names: Calasso, Roberto, author. | Parks, Tim, translator.
Title: The tablet of destinies / Roberto Calasso ; translated from the Italian by
    Tim Parks.
Other titles: Tavoletta dei destini. English
Description: First American edition. | New York : Farrar, Straus and Giroux,
    2022. | Includes index.
Identifiers: LCCN 2021062158 | ISBN 9780374605018 (hardcover)
Subjects: LCSH: Utnapishtim (Mythological character)—Fiction. |
    LCGFT: Epic fiction. | Novels.
Classification: LCC PQ4863.A3818 T3913 2022 | DDC 853/.914—dc23
LC record available at https://lccn.loc.gov/2021062158

www.fsgbooks.com
www.twitter.com/fsgbooks • www.facebook.com/fsgbooks

10   9   8   7   6   5   4   3   2   1

# CONTENTS

I

This storm was like no other he had known. Shipwrecks he was used to. They marked time, served as reminders. A certain event had happened before the third shipwreck, another after the fifth. Far from dismayed, what he felt was a strange, drunken recklessness, relief almost. Not only had he lost his course, the compass points themselves had disappeared. That was his last exact observation. He knew nothing of what happened next, until the moment when he opened his eyes in a tent. A light breeze stirred the fabric. He had slept, but for how long? Days? Years? In the darkness he recognized a shape. Stretched out, motionless. Another sleeper. For a while Sindbad said nothing. Then the other woke, looked at him, and said:

"This is the home of Utnapishtim, in Dilmun."

Utnapishtim got up and parted the flaps of the tent. In came a blade of light that lay beside Sindbad. Utnapishtim sat on a stool beside him and said:

"I know who you are. There's no need to say anything. If you want to listen to me, I'll be here."

Then everything grew muddled for Sindbad. When he woke

again he had an impression of great clarity. Utnapishtim was still sitting on the stool. He said:

"I've been silent so long I don't know where to start. Anywhere would do. But ancient custom has it that everything begins with the gods."

There was a brief silence. Then the voice resumed:

"In the beginning the gods walked the earth. They kept themselves busy. They dug ditches, raised up walls. Most of all, they searched for water. It was hard going. They felt oppressed by a heavy yoke. Not all the gods were equal. There were higher gods and lower gods. The Anunnaki had withdrawn to the heavens. They had left the Igigi to struggle on earth. One day they were bound to rebel. Men would learn from them. The Igigi dug out the bed of the Tigris. They grumbled among the heaps of earth they had turned up. Ever more exasperated. What could they do but take arms, attack the sky? Enlil the warrior, the counselor, was roused from his bed. They barred all the doors. They begged help of Anu, who had power over the heavens, and from Ea, deep in the fresh subterranean waters. Enlil wept. He didn't know what to do. Anu said the Igigi were right. Their lives were too hard, their outcry could be heard in the highest heaven.

"Then the gods realized they must create *substitutes* for themselves: men. But how? For them to be truly alive, a god must die. Mami, the midwife, could mix some clay with the blood of the god called Geshtue. The other gods would purify themselves, three times in a month, immersed in water. A spirit penetrated the clay with Geshtue's blood. And the clay began to throb. From then on, the spirit remembered the god he had belonged to.

"Mami went into the chamber of destiny, together with Ea. She began to knead the clay, streaked with blood. And whispered one of her spells, for she had once been a sorceress. Seven lumps of clay to the right, seven to the left. They became men and women. Now she placed a mud brick in the middle. Where we come from everything begins with mud bricks. She cut it in half with a piece of bamboo and, one by one, placed the lumps of clay beside each other. Nothing else was required. Soon afterward, those shapeless pieces of clay began to mate. Ishtar watched and was pleased.

"It was Ea, my protector, who explained to the Anunnaki what they must do. Ea had always been the most farsighted. Left to their own devices, the Anunnaki would have become mired in endless conflicts. But Ea spoke the crucial words: 'Let men carry the gods' burden!' Simple words that we still live by. That you, Sindbad, live by. They spell out the basics: the burden, the gods. All else is superfluous.

"Of Geshtue, I shall say very little. His name means 'ear,' no memorable deeds are attributed to him. But I do know he was thought *intelligent*. Perhaps that was why he was chosen. They killed him, all acting together, during the Anunnaki council. They shed blood together and together they purified themselves in water. The water of Ea.

"I have never understood why a god had to be killed in order for men to exist. In any event, it wasn't Ea who suggested it. All he said was that some creature had to be found who could *take the place* of the gods. But the Anunnaki were all in favor of the killing. And the deed had to be done in a particular place: along the Durmahu, the bond, the rope, the axis that ties the heavens to the earth. I heard this from the seven Apkallu, the

Holy Carp, the Seven Sages of Ea, who were close relatives of mine.

"I have told you these stories of the gods and the burdens because, when you lived in Baghdad, before you met Sindbad the Sailor, they called you Sindbad the Porter. You went around all day with heavy burdens on your head. Moving merchandise from one place to another. It was your whole life."

II

Sindbad was befuddled again. He heard strange names, for-eign sounds. And someone was speaking as though he knew every detail of his life. He couldn't see why these stories were so urgent. He would have preferred to be told where he was. He looked around and thought:

"All the ports I've seen, the dives, the taverns, markets and brothels and palaces . . . yet never anything like this Dilmun, a name I never came across on any nautical chart. Everything here could easily be found elsewhere, were it not for the bright-ness of the light. And the feeling that it might all melt away from one moment to the next."

Utnapishtim resumed his tale:

"The Flood didn't come suddenly as a big surprise. It came at the end of a long, tormented story. Men just went on multi-plying and the noise they made was ever more irksome. The Anunnaki summoned Namtar, who governs the things of death. 'Quieten down that noise,' they told him. And they asked him

to send a plague upon the earth. It was then that Ea told me something I didn't believe at first. At the four corners of the earth, the heralds were to whip men up, to have them make even more noise, stop showing the gods any reverence at all. Ea was the only god capable of speaking against the gods. But the Anunnaki were incensed. If the plague wasn't enough, they would send a famine. The rain ceased to fall. Everything dried up. The land seemed like it was covered in salt. People started to look daggers at one another. Spied on one another. Some mothers ate their daughters. And there were daughters who ate their mothers. I remember days of desperation. I spoke for hours, down by the bamboo, to Ea. And got no answer. So I took my bed to the riverbank. I waited for that time of night when everything would fall silent and the only sound was the water. Ea's voice would come from there.

"You're wondering: how did I talk to Ea? They said I had an ear for him, as if others found this path blocked. I heard his words as distinctly as I hear yours, and recognized at once that it was him. His voice was like no other. What about when it was my turn to speak? I remember a time when I lived in a big hut with bamboo walls. Close-woven, thick. I would sit facing one of these walls and talk in a low voice, like an idiot. Often there was no response. But sometimes Ea would answer, I heard him right there in front of me. It's the same now when we talk together. Ea never used my name. He spoke to the wall. He said: 'Bamboo! Bamboo! Listen up!' I was on the other side, in the dark, and I listened.

"Where I'm from, to say *watch out* we would say *listen*. We had the habit of listening more than seeing. I don't know if that's still the case. Our heads were empty thrones where

voices, shapes, and vibrations thronged together. Only when Ea brought me here, to Dilmun, did I discover the marvel of something that lets itself be seen, but makes no sound. There was nothing else to keep me company.

"The ravages of famine weren't enough for the Anunnaki. They were forever in council. They kept swearing they would act in unison, as though they themselves were the first to doubt it. But there was one exception. Sitting in his corner, like a guest who has just arrived, one day Ea burst out laughing.

"Enlil was ever more enraged and announced the Flood. What could the others do but agree? Then Ea recomposed himself and said something frightening: 'Can I raise my hand against those I have created?' It was a way of reminding the Anunnaki that only he and Mami had been present in the chamber of destiny. And that the underground waters depended on him.

"So the Flood was decided on and brought about without Ea's support. A punishment that would level everything in a vast expanse of mud. But Ea warned me in time for me to build the ship that was our salvation. This is common knowledge. What many don't know is that before building the ship, Ea sent me on a secret mission to my hometown: Shuruppak. Only Ea could calculate how far the waters would reach. And in a ditch in Shuruppak I hid the scriptures, those clay tablets that would bear witness to what happened *before* the Flood. Few know this part of the story. Those whose task it is to pass on the scriptures. Of whom you, Sindbad, are only the most recent.

"Nobody now remembers the exact details of the Flood. And details are useful. First the Anunnaki went all over the place carrying torches and setting fire to everything they could find. But then, when huge volumes of water began to fall from

the sky, one after another, and the earth was reduced to silence, the Anunnaki were so terrified they ended up huddling away in the heavens like so many dogs. They hadn't fully realized what was about to happen. The first to complain was Mami, who had fashioned the first men. She yelled something that the other Anunnaki had thought but hadn't dared to say: how could they have agreed to swear that the earth must be devastated by the Flood?

"If there had been no Flood, I could have gone on being one smart man among many. And Ea's favorite. I had no ambitions beyond that. But the Flood did come, on a rash whim of Enlil's. The Anunnaki soon regretted it. So Ea ordered me to build a strange square-shaped ship, sealed like a strongbox and packed full of animals. I didn't know where to begin, but Ea drew plans on the sand to teach me the shipbuilder's craft. So, when it was over, men and women found the land again. Not me, though; I vanished to a place that I alone inhabit: Dilmun. A magnificent place, but far removed from all other life. That's why they called me Utnapishtim the Remote. I have no one to talk to. You are the first visitor I've been able to speak to about all this since Gilgamesh.

"When Enlil saw the ship aground on the back of Mount Nimush he was seized by another fit of rage. Had it all been for nothing, then? Wasn't even the Flood enough? And who could have conspired against him? There was only one suspect: Ea, he who knows. As they said.

"In a flash Enlil changed. It's a privilege the gods enjoy. With solemn step, he climbed aboard the ship, took my hand, had me kneel together with my wife, touched us on the forehead, in blessing, and said: 'Utnapishtim, until today you have

been a man, from now on you and your wife will be like gods. And you will dwell at the confluence of the rivers.' From that moment on, I knew that life for me would never end. But I still wonder what it means to be *like* gods. How much like them? On the other hand, I know all too well what keeps me far from men. And I still yearn for what I have lost. Which is why I can't stop speaking to you, Sindbad."

"How did the Anunnaki behave after the Flood? Did they accept the existence of men? They chose not to say. They had killed men like flies and like flies they buzzed around the first sacrifice I celebrated as soon as I was off the ship. And Anu gave Nintu—another name for Mami—a necklace of lapis lazuli stones shaped like flies. She said she would never take it off, in memory of those calamitous days."

Darkness had fallen. Sindbad's mind wandered. Then once again, from the shadows, he heard Utnapishtim's voice: "I would have liked to be someone who dwells in the midst of everything and sees afar. Instead, my fate has been to see afar, but from a place no one else can reach. Or only you, Sindbad, and you weren't even looking for it."

III

"In the sky Ishtar is Venus, the brightest star at dawn and dusk, but among the fixed stars she is the goddess with the bow, in the constellation of the Great Dog, close to her lover Dumuzi, the true shepherd of the heavens, in Orion, and to Ninurta, the great hero, where the hurricane brews, who is Sirius, the arrow. Ishtar was other things as well. Where you see two parallel stands of bamboo, bending at the tips, or rosettes, or eight-pointed stars, you are seeing Ishtar. Sometimes her frilly skirts fall to her ankles. Sometimes she's quite naked, with wings, pushing up prosperous breasts, her feet on a lion, a two-horned crown on her head. It's still Ishtar. Taking the god's place, the king coupled with Ishtar in a room with a golden table and a bed with linen sheets. The king had been specially chosen to give the goddess sensual pleasure. Head high, he drew near to Ishtar's legs. She stretched her pure legs on the bed and on that bed the king pleasured her flesh. He was the beloved groom.

"It was an idea of Ea's, at once delicate and decisive, to seek out the Anunnaki and share the *mes*, the powers, with them, showing how and to what extent they could be used. All the

Anunnaki approved, drunk on power. Only when it came to Ishtar was there some turbulence in attributing the *mes*. But this was because Ishtar was the only one who could be everywhere at once. Other gods presided over single regions. Ishtar was imperial. She was present in every nook and cranny, permeated every surface. They called her *the girl who laughs with a happy heart*, but she was also one who fomented fighting and slaughter. No one could be sure what Ishtar would be from one moment to the next. Her turbulence upset every equilibrium. When Ea shared out the *mes* among the Anunnaki, Ishtar felt left out. She saw she hadn't been given a function for herself. She was sovereign, but without presiding over anything in particular. Now she was forced to realize that the only thing that was strictly hers was sexual pleasure. And even if no one was ready to forgo it, that pleasure served no purpose. The gods shared out territories and governments; she alone was everywhere and nowhere. Rather than any particular god, she resembled the divine, that embraces all and cannot be pinned down.

"Ea always avoided conflict. He knew nothing is ever settled by arguing. But Ishtar was furious, crushing everything in her path. So Ea resorted to an old trick. He made a Double of Ishtar. The goddess would have to fight it out with that. From the secret waters of the Apsu a powerful figure emerged, a warrior. Standing tall, headstrong. Ea called her Saltu, which means 'Quarrel.' If Ishtar wanted war among the gods, she would first have to fight Saltu, who resembled her more than any other creature. And so it was. This was one of the occasions when Ea revealed all his wisdom.

"We don't know who won the clash between Ishtar and her Double, which must have been something like a duel with a

mirror. But it was enough to cause quakes and crevasses everywhere. I remember that after a while silence fell. But Ishtar hadn't had her fill. She was hatching a plan.

"Wrapped in a cloak only gods possess, she climbed on the Boat of Heaven and chose to descend to the Apsu to visit Ea. Many saw her on the last leg of the journey, between Kulaba, her home in Uruk, and Eridu, where you go down to the Apsu.

"She said she wanted to speak, her alone, him alone, to Ea. 'Behold the silvery Ishtar, my daughter,' are words many of the guardians heard Ea pronounce. Just before they shut themselves up in a room of the subterranean palace, some of the dignitaries managed to glimpse their passing. A dazzling vision, they said. Huge luminous wings hovered over the boundless waters of the Apsu, opening the way for the goddess. No one would witness what followed, save, for a few moments, the servants who brought them food and drink. Exquisite no doubt. They whispered that Ea seemed drunk. They heard him say over and over: 'My daughter, my daughter.' And the two kept lifting bronze goblets. As for Ishtar's splendor, they didn't dare so much as begin to describe it. I feel sure they were telling the truth.

"No one knows drunkenness better than Ea. It was he who brought it to the gods. I know because he also revealed it to me. It was his secret gift. If it hadn't been for that gift, I would never have been able to stay here, alone among the palm trees.

"What did father and daughter talk about, all day and night? Those days and nights, rather. No one can say. All we know is that Ishtar left laden with gifts. A hundred and five powers. She looked on with a stern gaze as they were placed one by one in the Boat of Heaven. But how could she see them? You mustn't

suppose that the powers were as they are now: invisible. On the contrary, they were often things that you could touch. Talismans, people used to call them. But what were those powers? And why were there so many?

"Let me list some of the most important for you: the power to go down to the Underworld and come back; the use of the sexual organs. Ea explained: wisdom in handling the phallus. Ishtar answered: 'I accept.' But that was only the beginning. There were many others: the art of working wood; the art of the scribe; attention; kindling fires; procreation; judgment; betrayal; deceit; black clothing; colored clothing; the banner; the quiver; the kiss; hypocrisy; the tavern; song; treachery; pillage; the lament; prosperity; architecture; the oblation; deference; lying; victory; makeup. And these are only some of those one hundred and five powers.

"When they had all been loaded on the Boat of Heaven, Ea awoke from the lethargy that had held him in its grip and showed his irritation. Had he given his daughter too much, perhaps? He immediately dispatched agents to recover at least some of the powers. All negotiation was in vain. Ishtar refused even to be involved, leaving her ever-faithful assistant Ninshubur to do the talking. And Ea's agents had to return empty-handed. What had Ishtar won from Ea? What I call *powers* were once called *mes*, a word that later lost its clarity. The *mes* are at once powers and laws. Or rules. A destiny. When Ishtar, who was still called Inanna then, went down to the Underworld, she was wearing seven *mes*. They included a crown, some jewels, a cloak. How can one hold a law or a power in one's hand? When a ceremony was performed without any mistakes, people said

that the *mes* had been accomplished. At the time, everyone understood perfectly what this meant. Now it is too late to explain. But that's how it was.

"At last, the Boat of Heaven reached Uruk. It came in through the Nigulla gate and was welcomed by a crowd who could scarcely believe their eyes: how could so many powers have invaded the town all at once, bringing such sparkle to life on earth henceforth?"

"The *mes* that Ishtar persuaded Ea to grant her were not restricted to regal or priestly emblems. True, these were at the top of the list, but after them came other *mes*, such as the art of tying and loosening a hair bun, of sacking a city, or of starting arguments, or disguising oneself. What was it that held them together?

"The list of *mes* included everything that the world of light, to which Ishtar was about to return, must not and could not do without. It was the imperishable fabric of appearance. And from the beginning, it included the capacity to come into contact with death and not to succumb. The *me* immediately before that was the truth.

"The *mes* were also norms, laws, rules. But before anything else they were manifestations that must belong to the path of life. If even one *me*, no matter how frivolous or ferocious, were to be missing, then order in the world would prove inadequate. And in fact order was always inadequate. Though it continued to be order, up to a point. Until something broke and everything fell apart. Then wise expedients needed to be found so

that everything could return to its proper place. This was the art of the gods. And Ea knew it better than the others."

"The hundred and five *mes* Ishtar took from Ea were not the only ones. There were any number of them. To possess the *mes* was to master all the patterning of life, down to the smallest trifle. And Inanna claimed to be queen of the *mes*, without limits.

"No one proclaimed this with such unique eloquence as Enheduanna, daughter of King Sargon and priestess of the moon god, Nanna, in Ur. Words spoken in tumultuous times. A rebellion was tearing the kingdom apart; it was led by Lugalanne, who claimed he had the favor of Nanna. More than the god of the moon, Enheduanna worshipped Ishtar. And she called on the goddess for protection against the impending onslaught. But what arms did she have at her disposal? Only the words she would use to evoke Ishtar. They had to be precise and explosive if the goddess were to respond.

"*Radiant light of the innumerable* mes. Such were the opening words of her invocation, etched in my mind as Enheduanna etched them in clay. Sometimes I recite them: *The* mes *are pressed to your breasts . . . You are a dragon spreading poison in enemy territory . . . A queen astride wild beasts, emanating terrible splendor . . . Your doings opened the gate of tears . . . Your teeth shatter granite . . . Like fluttering bats, the Anunnaki flee before you, hiding in heaps of rubble . . . The rebels cannot resist your lethal gaze . . . Who could ever appease your heart? . . . You are taller than the heavens, who could ever overthrow you? . . . They must know how you crush their heads . . . My queen, brimming beauty, glory itself.*

"Ishtar must have been pleased with these words. Perhaps no one had *written* words like this before. Yet Enheduanna was hounded from the temple and flew off like a swallow. War raged. Lugalanne still felt he had the protection of the moon god. But it wasn't enough. Nothing is enough against Ishtar."

"Ishtar didn't just possess the *mes*, she used them. Her word easily became action. It was another reason Ishtar was so attractive and so terrifying. When she moved, she could unleash all things extreme. If you came close to her, everything would vibrate. That could happen facing an enemy or just in the touching of two bodies. Without Ishtar, no moment could achieve the solidity and brilliance of metal."

Sindbad had a question:

"Whenever I returned from one of my seven journeys and recounted my adventures there was always someone who agreed, then with a slight shake of the head would say: 'You can't escape destiny.' At first, happily ingenuous as I was, I didn't understand. But there came the moment when I thought I had understood. And now, having reached, without even trying to, the place whence Ea, your protector god, set out one day in a ship to fix the destinies of many places, I wonder what I had understood exactly. I wonder whether those places had no destiny before Ea passed by."

Utnapishtim answered at once:

"Yes, all that did happen. Ea's ship was called *The Apsu Goat*. Each power has its origins in the waters of the Apsu. Including

the power over destinies. Ea used to say he was the lord of destinies. I remember Ninagirsig, the commander of the *Goat*, when he raised his golden wand and the sailors' oars, in perfect time, stirred the waters of the sacred lagoon. It was a glorious moment.

"Some of the stories I'm telling happened after I had already arrived here in Dilmun, others I'd heard even before Ea saved me on the box-shaped ship, along with the animals. Some are stories I was involved in myself. A minor player. But as time goes by, such distinctions fade and dissolve. The stories link up with one another, as if they knew their places from the start. And I move from one to another as though along a single glittering belt. In the end, they're just stories. And you don't ask a story to show its papers.

"Having lived here in Dilmun for a few thousand years now, I can say that the first stories you need to know are those of Ea and Ishtar. In ancient times they were called Enki and Inanna. Sometimes I still call them that. Other stories are not so intricate and don't go so far back. But with these, I'm never sure I've understood their deepest meaning. Yet Ea is my protector, and he called Ishtar his daughter. I have never been so close to anyone else. As for the Anunnaki, I couldn't really say where they're to be found these days. A fog has come down. Ea made me like them. Now it's they who are like me. No one visits them, as no one has visited me since Gilgamesh. Until you came along, Sindbad."

Sindbad was eager to explore Dilmun. He disappeared on long expeditions, returning after dark. He never asked about

anything. Once he came back when night was almost over, distraught. Utnapishtim was awake. Sindbad sat facing him and was silent for a while. Then he said:

"There are many who think I did nothing all my life but travel. Some just called me 'The Sailor.' For sure, I have seen any number of marvels and monstrosities. But today I saw something I don't even have a name for. I went farther than usual; around me, everything was pleasantly humdrum. Suddenly I realized I was on the edge of something different. It was still light, a translucent light. Before me, in every direction, lay an expanse packed with hundreds of cone-shaped mounds, of sand and earth, all the same size and the same color, all the same distance, one from the next. There were hundreds—thousands rather, because it seemed they stretched off beyond the horizon. It wasn't the desert, but nor did it seem a place where men ever went. There was an order, but what kind of order? It was like seeing a sequence of numbers made visible. I had the impression I was *seeing time*. Nothing of the kind ever happened to me before. At first, I felt terror, then a light, crazy euphoria. Then again terror.

"I couldn't move. When night fell, I managed a few steps and immediately lost all sense of direction. At a certain point, in the dark, I found myself facing an even darker barrier. A dense wall of date palms. I began to breathe and, with some difficulty, managed to find my way back to our tent."

Utnapishtim had listened as if he were aware of everything Sindbad was about to say before he said it. When Sindbad finished Utnapishtim said:

"Now you know what Dilmun is."

IV

"When she was still called Inanna, Ishtar had desired to leave the Great Above and go down to the Great Below to see her older sister Ereshkigal, who was queen there. The Anunnaki were appalled. They were staid gods who never did more than pass from one to another of their temples, on certain days, in nine cities, all contained between the two great rivers. They knew nothing of travel. The very idea would have been abhorrent. For Inanna, war itself was a kind of travel. Every battle was one stage of a larger exploration, a drive to expand her territory. Now she had decided to descend to the one place whence no return is permitted.

"Inanna said she wanted to go down to the Underworld to take part in the funeral rites for the Bull of Heaven, Ereshkigal's husband, whom Gilgamesh and Enkidu had killed and cut to pieces. But that was an alibi. You can't kill a constellation.

"All Inanna really wanted was to set foot in the Underworld. And come back. Then she could say the Underworld was part of her territory. Only the rash and insolent Inanna could have thought she could go to see Ereshkigal as if it were no more

than a family visit. Gorgeously made up, with earrings, neck-laces, bracelets, rings, corset, and cloak—all *mes* designed to ward off attacks—Inanna set forth. She came to seven gates whose bars were thick with dust. At each gate, she had to sur-render one of her ornaments, her powers. When at last Inanna entered her sister Ereshkigal's kingdom, she had no defenses left. No one knows what happened next. She reappeared hang-ing from a butcher's hook like a carcass. Naked, dead—and so she remained for three days and three nights. None of the su-preme gods felt inclined to go to her aid, except Ea, who quickly fashioned two demons to take her water and wine to revive her. They told her she could return to the place whence she had descended. She would be escorted by the Galla, seven demons like sharp-pointed canes. But there was a condition: a substi-tute must take her place in the Underworld, forever. The first to come to meet her was the faithful Ninshubur, her protecting shadow. Bowing to the ground, Ninshubur at once offered her-self as Inanna's substitute. The demons would have agreed. Not Inanna, though; she didn't want to lose Ninshubur's precious help. It was thanks to her that her *mes* were saved when Ea had wanted to take them back. The same thing happened with Shara, Inanna's hairdresser and poet. 'I will never let you have him,' Inanna told the Galla. And again with Lulal, her shield bearer. Inanna couldn't do without these loyal supporters and their skills.

"Finally, they came to the Great Apple Tree, in Kulaba, the part of Uruk where Inanna usually lived. There were shepherds playing their flutes. Dumuzi was sitting, motionless. Facing a large stage. Apparently unperturbed. But how could he be un-aware of his lover's predicament? Had he forgotten her? Inanna's

eyes looked daggers. She said: 'He's the one, take him!' The Galla quickly grabbed him by the legs. They tied him up and beat him. Dumuzi called on Utu, the Sun, to save him. He slipped through the Galla's hands like a snake. And took refuge with his sister, Geshtinanna. But the Galla found him and caught him again. He couldn't escape. Dumuzi ceased to be Inanna's lover and became her substitute in the Underworld. Inanna herself had chosen him.

"The one goal of the seven Galla demons was to capture more and more inhabitants for the Underworld. For them the young god Dumuzi was the most precious of prizes. They tormented him, pursued him, laid siege to him, yet were never sated. They wanted him dead. In the end, Dumuzi was trapped and killed in the place where he felt most at home: his shepherd's hut.

"They covered his lifeless body with a linen cloth, like a basket of dates. Next to it there was a dog, who ate something, then curled up at Dumuzi's feet. There was a crow in the hut as well. And the crow, too, was eating something. Then it flew off. In the night, Inanna came. She repeated the same words over and over: 'Oh, you who lie here, you watched over me!' She left a gift by the body stretched on the ground: a goatskin full of water. 'Essential in the desert,' Inanna muttered to herself."

"Inanna and Dumuzi's story had begun with a linen sheet. Small or large, it's something you have to have, Inanna's brother, Utu, the Sun, told her. Right, said Inanna, but it will have to be spun, woven, whitened. Who is going to do that? I'll handle it, said Utu. And when I've got this wedding sheet, asked Inanna,

who's going to get under it with me? Dumuzi the shepherd, Utu replied. No, said Inanna, I don't want a shepherd. Their wool is coarse. A farmer would offer a lot more. But Utu talked about the shepherd's tasty cream. And Dumuzi was Ea's son. In the end, Inanna rubbed herself with perfumed oil, put on her necklace of lapis lazuli, picked up her seal, and opened the door. Moonlight filtered from the room. Dumuzi came in, bearing a bowl of thick cream. Inanna spread the linen sheet on the bed."

"Descending to the Underworld, Inanna threw down a challenge no other god had dared to make. But the result was her first and only defeat. Those three days and nights hanging ignominiously from a meat hook in a place crawling with feathered, dust-eating larvae amounted to a last warning. No longer would she be able to proclaim her unlimited capacity for expansion. But for the other gods, too, her descent to the Underworld opened wounds that would never heal. In the past, they had thought to fashion men as their substitutes. It was a strategy that lightened their burden without requiring any great effort. All they had to do was kill a rather obscure god and mix his blood with some clay.

"Now everything was different. If the gods meant to expand to encompass everything, they could no longer deny the fact that the Underworld was beyond them. They could not cohabit with death and the dead. And this left them diminished. They refused even to talk about it. The Anunnaki realized they were gods only up to a point.

"Substitution had insinuated itself among the gods. It was

no longer merely an expedient to make life easier and more powerful. It was also the breach that death had opened among the gods. Nor did it change much that Dumuzi had to spend only half the year in the Underworld thanks to his sister Geshtinanna's willingness to sacrifice herself and substitute for him. Geshtinanna was also a child of Ea's, hence a divine being. And Inanna would have to acknowledge that the hundred and five *mes* she had taken from Ea when he was drunk did not give her power over everything. Death was impervious to them. Something else was required: a substitute, a living being.

"If life were to expand to its furthest limits, substitution was a must, but substitution brought death. Or rather, it was death that brought about substitution. Whether as killing or disappearance."

"The gods were not the only ones devoted to order; so were men, or Black Heads, as they were called. They studied what went on, whatever went on, seeking out omens. Ill omens for the most part. Their kings lived in perpetual fear of an eclipse or a misshapen liver or an abnormal birth.

"When order was threatened, they, too, saw substitution as a necessary expedient. If some ill omen cast a shadow on the king—astral events were always the most frightening—a substitute had to be found to take his place at all regal functions, hold his scepter, sit on his throne, sleep in his bed, beside a queen, who was also a substitute. Meanwhile the real king disappeared to a safe place known only to a very few. This state of affairs would go on for a while, but not too long, until a prophetess or a

minister of court announced to the substitute that he must meet his destiny. Meaning, in his case, that he was to be killed. And his temporary queen with him.

"After which, solemn funerals were held. When at last the substitute was about to be buried, people whispered: 'Take all evils down to the land of no return.'"

"The Black Heads were forever tormented by the fear that something, anything they did might upset one of the Anunnaki and arouse their hostility. The gods were not remote; on the contrary, they were too close for comfort. You had to protect yourself behind a barrier of prayers, invocations, exorcisms. Such gestures were never superfluous; they marked the hours day by day.

"On the other hand, the fact that the Anunnaki were so present exposed them to certain mishaps. Even Ishtar, sovereign of sovereigns, had to come to terms with this. In general, the Anunnaki paid attention only to things that had specifically to do with them, rites and ceremonies. The occasional war. Aside from Ea, Ishtar was the only one who was interested in everything that went on on earth. It wasn't beyond her to come down from the mountains, from Elam, from Subir, like some mysterious stranger, wrapped in her royal cloak.

"But then someone would recognize her and the rumor would get around: 'Ishtar is among us, she could appear anytime.' She rode astride a lion, who had once been her lover. She looked around her, seeking to sound out men's hearts. Not to bring justice, which was hardly her job. She just wanted to tell true from false. And maybe find another lover or two. She

had had the hoopoe, the horse, the wolf—so why not a man? But with men there was always a chance something could go wrong; it had happened in the past already, and with Dumuzi, too, the shepherd, the only one of her lovers whom everyone remembered and periodically mourned. But Dumuzi was a god.

"One day Ishtar saw a row of poplars by the river, shady, stirring in the wind. Trees, to Ishtar, were replicas of herself. The goddess spread her cloak in this enchanting place and fell asleep.

"Someone was watching. Shukaletuda, the gardener. After many failed attempts, he had managed to plant those trees in the only place they would grow, while all around everything was arid. Young and thoughtful, Shukaletuda was a loner. He observed the sky and studied it. Became an expert in demons and wandering spirits. He even strove to decipher the destinies laid down by the Anunnaki.

"He often stopped by his poplars; it was the place he loved best. One day he saw a woman's body stretched out on a cloak. She radiated brightness. A slim belt, adorned with the talismans of her seven powers, was fastened around her waist. With the utmost skill and circumspection, Shukaletuda removed the powers one by one and penetrated the sleeping woman. Then he went back to his observation point and hid.

"Waking up, Ishtar saw that her belt with its talismans had been undone. In the wells all around water turned to blood. Ishtar searched for the person who had defiled her. Shukaletuda had taken refuge with his father, Ea, who advised him to blend in with the crowd, where it was most dense. 'She won't find you, you'll see,' Ea had said. Even as he spoke, the city was hit by a whirlwind of scorching sand that Ishtar had stirred up.

"But Shukaletuda was not to be found. So Ishtar turned to Ea, who was her father too, and who had always helped her. Livid, she demanded he give up Shukaletuda. She would take him by the hand and shut herself up together with him in her temple, in Eridu. After all, she said, they were brother and sister. So it was. Ishtar and Shukaletuda entered the sanctuary together, in silence. No one knows what happened inside. All that was heard were these few words of Ishtar's: 'Whatever the fate that awaits you, your name will not be forgotten, the poets will sing of you.' Shukaletuda was never seen again. And today I am repeating his name."

V

"For a long time the only ones who visited me were the seven Apkallu, the Holy Carp. They slid out of the water together like a dance troupe, their scales gleaming gray and purple, with the heads of wise men. Speaking with them was like watching the earth from Ursa Major. Then all at once they would slide back into the water.

"At last the wind blew from the valley of the Indus, that wind written in your name: *sind bad*. You came from the sea, not from the lagoon. You are salty with seawater. I live at the point where the fresh waters spring up from the deep and mingle at the confluence of the rivers. We speak languages from different families, though both worship what is liquid. You traveled far to reach this place, unaware. I expected you from the start. I yearned to feel this other wind, blowing from places that know nothing of the Anunnaki and celebrate other gods that the Anunnaki know nothing of. I am fascinated by this confusion, this mixing of names and languages, something always about to happen and never finally accomplished.

"One day the Anunnaki withdrew. Where they went I don't

know. They had homes in the stars. And their name means: Children of Heaven. As for me, very likely they forgot me. Or wanted me to stay put where I was. In the end, I was always a relic.

"The thing I know best is the thing that most resists man's knowing: my protector god, Ea. I can't pretend to be an expert on anything else. The first thing that has to be said about Ea is that his kingdom cannot be seen. A boundless subterranean stratum of fresh water: the Apsu. Beneath that water, a staircase leads down to the kingdom of Ereshkigal. Where the dead are.

"From the beginning, Ea's home was apart and remote from that of the other gods. The waters rise in two spouts from his shoulders. Umsu, his minister, has two faces and looks very like his master. They wear the same hat, with four parallel pairs of horns. But the waters do not gush from his shoulders.

"There was a time when everyone knew these stories. They introduced variations, they superimposed one on another, or combined them, or split them up. And etched them on clay tablets. The tablets ended up buried under rubble and sand. Thousands upon thousands of them. In the end, I was the only one left who knew those stories. But I had no one to tell them to, until you arrived. From that moment on, I haven't been able to stop telling them once again, even when you're sleeping. Nothing I tell you is made up. It all happened. Or at least, it was all etched on those clay tablets."

At this point Sindbad interrupted:

"In the ports I passed through, people didn't tell stories about gods. They didn't feel the need. They told stories about merchants and warriors, princesses and prostitutes, peasants and administrators, cultured men and sages, as well as kings

and queens. But every now and then, there would be stories quite unlike any of these. And they lodged themselves in the mind, they came back at night. One of those stories has tormented me for years. All I can say is that I came across it in a very remote place, in the Tropics. And it has never left me.

"A man like any other, recently married and living with his wife's relatives. They were suspicious of him. One night, the rain began to drum on the leaves. The hut seemed to rise up into the sky, held there by that lovely sound. The man looked at his beautiful wife, whom he had touched only a few times as yet, and said: 'We could sleep under the rain.' They were words of love: his first, and as it turned out his last. The woman scowled and didn't reply. The man turned toward the forest again, imagining they were alone, and said: 'I would like to learn the rain song.' But his brothers-in-law were spying on him. From the darkness of the hut, together with their sisters, they watched the man's movements as he listened to the torrential rain. In a low voice, the woman had told them: 'He wants to sleep under the rain.' And added: 'He must be joking.' Silence fell, a heavy silence. Then, an evil glint in his eyes, one of the brothers said, 'Fine, if he wants to learn that song, he'd better do it now . . .'

"Come the dawn, the man was exhausted from the pleasure the rain had brought him. His wife and brothers-in-law leaped on him; they were needlessly brutal. They dragged him outside and tied him to a post that was part of an old abandoned house. The rain fell without a break. All day and all night the drops beat down on him. He had the impression his body was riddled with holes from the water. He was delirious. At the same time and in great detail his mind was elaborating the plan he would put into action were he to survive. The rain that had

been his most exquisite pleasure went on torturing him with no respite. The only parts of his body he could feel were a few shreds of mosquito-bitten skin. When dawn came, his wife and brothers-in-law returned and untied him. The man was all but dead. He didn't say a word. They never spoke of that night again. Little by little, the man recovered his strength. Now he could go hunting again.

"He said to his wife: 'Come hunting with me. It's been a while since we ate meat.' And he began weaving a big wicker basket to carry the game. He asked his wife to crouch down so he could take the measurements for his basket. 'It'll need to be big, this time,' he muttered to himself. When he had finished, he asked his wife to get in the basket to check it was the right size. The wife got in and it fit like a glove. Then the man tied his wife's hands and feet and she heard him explain: 'When I said I wanted to sleep under the rain I meant that I wanted your body. Now I am going to smoke you, I shall cut you to pieces and serve your tasty flesh to your parents, your brothers, and your sisters. Don't yell out now, as I didn't yell out under the rain.' The man cooked his wife on a low flame. Then he cut her up as one cuts up an animal. He mixed the flesh with pieces of peccary meat and other game that he had killed hunting. At the bottom of the basket, he left his wife's feet together with her bracelets, necklaces, and earrings. On top was her liver.

"The woman's relatives hadn't eaten meat for a long time. They found the chunks piled in the basket delicious. They grabbed with greedy hands. At last, in the bottom of the basket, they found the woman's feet, her rings and bracelets. Her mother said: 'I have eaten my daughter. Get the knives and kill her husband.'

"But the man was gone. While his in-laws were eating, he had said: 'I'm just off to look for my wife. Perhaps the basket she's carrying is too heavy for her.' They pursued him for years. The man fled through the forest, where his brothers-in-law found the remnants of his campfires. At first they were cold and windblown. Gradually they got closer and closer. Now they were finding warm ashes. One day they caught sight of the man climbing into a canoe to get away. He already had one foot in the boat and one leg in the air when a brother-in-law's axe hacked it right off. The man fell into the canoe and drifted out onto the water. Bleeding heavily, he thought: 'So now what can I turn myself into? If I become a fish, they will fish for me. If I become an animal, they will hunt me down and eat me.' Lying on the bottom of the canoe, he lifted his eyes to the sky. 'Up there, I'll go up there,' he said. 'They'll never catch me there.' So the man ascended to the constellation of Orion, where at last he had a name: the one-legged hunter."

VI

"Like a pool of light sunk in a broader light, certain images come back: Gilgamesh and Enkidu build a raft and load it with a cedar trunk from Humbaba's forest. Enkidu is at the helm. Sitting on the trunk, Gilgamesh is holding Humbaba's head, now bereft of its powerful auras. That is the moment it begins, before everything falls apart. And Gilgamesh reaches my abode, alone."

"Gilgamesh would never have confronted Humbaba if he hadn't been with Enkidu, the man of the forest whom he had fought the first time he saw him, only to realize that he loved him more than anyone else.

"The animals of the forest saw Enkidu as one of their own. They would meet at the watering hole, without troubling one another. A form of benign, mutual disregard. This changed forever when Shamhat appeared. A prostitute of rare beauty. Enkidu was dazzled. More than Shamhat's body, it was her makeup, her jewels, her perfume that stunned him. There was

a new animal in the forest. They coupled for seven days and seven nights, without a break. For Enkidu it was a long journey through unknown territory. Pure pleasure was alien to the forest, where coupling was like eating, drinking, or sleeping.

"The animals sensed at once that something had changed forever between themselves and Enkidu. They stayed away from him. The gazelles fled. He had become a stranger, even before Shamhat took his hand, covered him with some of her clothes, and led him to a place Enkidu had never seen: Uruk, the Great City.

"Enkidu and Shamhat entered Uruk together. They were inseparable now. Enkidu was only slightly less tall than Gilgamesh and radiated strength and beauty just as he did. His chest was massive and hairy, his body wrapped in glittering clothes hardly suitable for a man. It was the first time he had seen a city, and for the inhabitants of Uruk it was the first time they had seen a being from the remote Cedar Forest in their streets."

"During their journey to the Cedar Forest, after more than a month's march, Enkidu built Gilgamesh a chamber for the god of dreams. They were at the top of a mountain and Gilgamesh had offered a libation, asking the mountain for a dream. So Enkidu prepared a suitable place for him to receive it. It was circular and had a door. Gilgamesh lay in the middle. For portents to appear you needed a closed place in the middle of the forest. As a man of the forest, Enkidu knew that. No one had taught him, but he was able to give the right advice.

"Many spoke of Humbaba as a monster. But he was a divine being who stayed away from the heavens because he preferred

the Cedar Forest. You can't kill a divine being in direct combat. You must approach him with dreams. That was the only thing that would work. That is why, when the two friends presented themselves to him, Humbaba felt betrayed by Enkidu and immediately said as much. The duel came as a consequence."

"Enkidu knew dreams and they proved fatal for him. One night he saw the gods meeting in council. They couldn't accept that a partly divine being had killed two entirely divine beings, Humbaba and the Bull of Heaven. They must be avenged. But which of the two killers should pay? Enkidu, they decided at once, son of a gazelle and a wild donkey. From silence he was born and to silence he must return.

"Enkidu wept and began to speak to the imposing door that he had made with wood from the Cedar Forest. He spoke to the door as if it were a person, recalling the long hours and the skill it had taken to fashion and adorn it. He had dedicated it to Enlil, who had prompted him to kill Humbaba and the Bull of Heaven, but Enlil had also been the first of the gods to demand Enkidu's death. Perhaps the door too had hoped to last forever, protected by the god to whom it belonged. Yet one day an enemy king would come along and destroy it. 'As is happening to me,' said Enkidu."

"The first exploit of Gilgamesh was the model of all exploits. He crossed six mountain ranges without finding the tree he wanted to cut down, a cedar. When he found it, on the seventh mountain range, he didn't say a word and looked no farther.

Using an axe forged specially for him in Uruk, he began to strike the tree. The young men who had come with him cut and stacked the branches. Gilgamesh went on mercilessly striking the trunk. The silence of the forest echoed with blows and thuds.

"Humbaba awoke. His weapons were terrifying auras. Gilgamesh, Enkidu, and their companions were seized by a sudden weariness. They could barely stand. One after the other they sank to the ground. The first to get up, much later, was Enkidu. He was born and bred in the forest, he knew its moods. And he knew Humbaba. Gilgamesh tried to get up too, but his feet were stuck to the ground. Humbaba was gurgling words that only Enkidu could understand. Before going back to Uruk, they would have to find out if Humbaba was a man or a god. 'Terror versus terror,' Gilgamesh said. 'Cunning versus cunning.'

"Gilgamesh was speaking in a void, because Humbaba didn't let them see him. He chose to start with cunning, offering two of his sisters, first Emmebaragni, then the younger Peshtur. The first trap is always a woman. Enkidu agreed. They should become relatives, Gilgamesh said, and share the auras of terror between them. But first he had to find Humbaba's hiding place in the dense forest. Otherwise, his wandering terror would spread farther and farther. After his sisters, Gilgamesh went on offering gifts to Humbaba: big sandals, small sandals, rock crystals, lapis lazuli, chalcedony. As if they were bartering at the market. Humbaba was still invisible, but for every gift he yielded up an aura. They appeared as long cedar trunks. Gilgamesh's companions immediately cut and stacked their branches.

"At last, Gilgamesh was closing in on Humbaba's lair. The comedy could unfold. He approached as though to kiss him but

instead struck him on the temple and tied him up with the help of two friends. Humbaba gnashed his teeth in rage. Then began to weep. He said he knew nothing but the forest. He didn't have a father or mother, but wanted at least to talk to Utu, the Sun.

"Gilgamesh would have freed him. His exploit was done. But Enkidu urged him not to. Humbaba, he said, would muddle up all the forest paths. No one would be able to get out. They had to kill him. Humbaba sensed the threat at once. So Gilgamesh thrust a knife in his throat. Then cut off his head and stuffed it in a leather sack. They went back the same way they'd come. And presented themselves to Enlil and his consort, Ninlil. They pulled Humbaba's head out of the leather bag.

"Enlil was furious. He had never ordered anyone to kill Humbaba, who was a god himself, after all. They should have sat down with Humbaba, broken bread with him, drunk some water together. But his rage didn't last long. Enlil was eager to get his hands on Humbaba's auras. So ended Gilgamesh's first exploit, model for all exploits.

"Gilgamesh never explained why he decided to kill Humbaba. And no one asked him. Humbaba was nothing less than a god, even though his parents had no name. They were a cave in the mountains. Humbaba possessed immense power and didn't use it. They called him the Living One. The gods thought of him as the guardian of the cedars. Gilgamesh had done something wicked. But in the end, the Anunnaki were quietly pleased. It meant one less power beyond their own."

"Only once was Ishtar turned down, by Gilgamesh. He mentioned her many lovers, who had all come to sorry ends. And

Gilgamesh was also the only one who began his exploits by cutting down a tree, a tree in the forest of the Living One, the terrific Humbaba with his seven magical powers. Gilgamesh had no plans to become the consort of a goddess, his ambition was to defeat death. He became aware of this one day when he leaned over the walls of Uruk and saw a corpse floating in the water, slowly drifting away. And he thought: 'That will be me soon enough.'"

"In those days, those long-ago days, those days when the heavens had only recently split from the earth, when Ishtar was still called Inanna, and Ea was still called Enki, at that time there was a solitary tree, a solitary willow, on the banks of the sacred Euphrates. It drank the water of the sacred Euphrates. It so happened that a powerful south wind uprooted the tree and broke its branches. Then Inanna gathered it up in her hands and planted it again in Uruk, in her pure garden. Inanna fed it with water that she had trodden in with her own feet.

"The willow grew strong again. Ten years passed. The Knowing Serpent consumed the willow at the base, the Thunderbird hid in its branches, a Demon Girl slid into its trunk. Little by little, the willow was eaten up by its three parasites. Inanna wept over its fate. Her brother Utu, who was also the Sun, offered no help.

"Then Gilgamesh turned up. He struck down the Knowing Serpent, forced the Thunderbird and the Demon Girl to flee. If something is eaten up, it is because an evil power is at work. Now the willow grew whole again. After which Gilgamesh and the young men of Uruk cut it down. He couldn't stop cutting

down trees, whether cedars or willows. And he couldn't avoid succumbing to death. With the blocks and planks Gilgamesh offered her, Inanna the goddess built her throne and her bed.

"Gilgamesh used what was left of the solitary willow to make a ball and stick. He went down to Uruk's main square and invited the local boys to join him in playing with the ball and stick. The girls watched and yelled. In the melee, the ball and stick fell into a crack in the ground. And ended up in the Underworld. Gilgamesh realized he would never be able to get them back. On the threshold of the Underworld, he sat down and wept. Saying: 'Oh, my ball! Oh, my stick, I didn't enjoy them to the full, didn't play with them enough!' Enkidu consoled him. He promised he would go down to the Underworld that very day and bring back the ball and the stick. Gilgamesh warned Enkidu to take care that the shades didn't recognize him. He mustn't wear sweet-smelling clothes, mustn't use perfume, mustn't wear sandals. Above all, he mustn't get close to shades he had loved or hated. Seven days went by and Enkidu hadn't come back. Then Gilgamesh wept for his faithful friend. He said: 'He didn't die in battle, on the field of men; the Underworld has snatched him away.'

"Desperate, Gilgamesh asked for help from more than one god, in vain. Only the knowing Ea came to his aid. And Enkidu's shade reappeared. Then Gilgamesh eagerly asked him how the Underworld was governed, what order prevailed, what fate awaited men? Did it depend on how they had lived on earth? Enkidu's answers read like articles of law. But no mention was made of the ball and stick."

"Twice Ishtar wept. The first time out of rage and vexation, because Gilgamesh had rejected her. The second time in her temple, because the solitary willow she had taken from the Euphrates was all eaten away. Gilgamesh was present on both occasions. First offending the goddess, then indulging her, but as a brother, not a lover.

"And twice Gilgamesh wept. Once because his ball and stick, made from the wood of the solitary willow, had vanished into the Underworld. Once for his friend Enkidu, who went down to the Underworld to get them back, never to return to the light above, except as a shade.

"Ishtar and Gilgamesh could be fierce opponents. But they are the only ones who are said to have seen the Deep. The waters of Ea. Such complicity went beyond hostility.

"Ishtar's throne and Gilgamesh's ball, which fell into the Underworld and led to Enkidu's death, were both made of the wood of the same willow. No bond could have been stronger."

"Gilgamesh came here as a stranger, a foreigner, standing tall in Urshanabi's boat. He was worn out, pale, distraught. He was punting the boat with a long pole. I saw a rag hanging from another pole, vertical on the boat. It was the first ever sail, I later discovered, made from the boatman's clothes. But only the faintest breeze blows over the waters of the dead. What matters is never to touch them. They are fatal.

"When Gilgamesh spoke to me, the first thing he talked about was the many risks he had run and the challenges he had faced to reach me. Every word reminded me of someone else, someone who spoke the same way: Ishtar. She was the only one

of the Anunnaki who told stories of the rivers and marshes and mountains she had crossed, of the icy cold and suffocating heat . that had oppressed and bruised her beauty. The goddess and the man who had refused to be her lover seemed to take turns at telling the same story. As if that story tied them tighter than the bed they hadn't shared.

"I knew it and dreaded it: I was the one who would have to explain to Gilgamesh that his adventures were to no avail. Man is as fleeting as the dragonfly that flits for a day over the waters of the Euphrates and is gone. It was a hateful task, but that was why the Anunnaki had given it to me.

"I did what I had to. Afterward I was pierced by the sharpest of pains. A moment of torment that has stayed with me ever since, and will be with me, I imagine, forever.

"Gilgamesh fell silent after I spoke. His eyes on the ground. Then he looked up and, in a voice so calm it was frightening, said: 'You are like me. There is no difference between us.' And he was right: on the one hand, a gaunt old man. On the other, a young man, a warrior perhaps, exhausted from battle. What could set them apart? A trick. It so happened that, after the Flood, I turned away from men and toward my protector, Ea. And became the one and only dweller in Dilmun. I hadn't warned the people who had boarded the box-shaped ship. They were left leaderless. And all, for all time, destined to die. Gilgamesh, too, one day."

"When Gilgamesh departed, like a gust of wind, he left me with a constant craving to speak of him. But to whom? Only one voice could talk back to me: the voice of Siduri, the alewife.

We lived on opposite banks of the waters of death, like neighbors in a vast prairie. On rare occasions, we were able to visit each other. It was I who went to her. I sat at the bar of her tavern, like any ordinary customer. I never tired of hearing her tell how she first saw Gilgamesh. He had arrived wrapped in a lion skin, like a hunter of wild bulls, rowdy, shaggy, and brusque.

"Siduri had barred the tavern door and fled to the roof for safety. When, finally, she agreed to serve at the bar, Gilgamesh sat facing her and began to boast of his exploits with Enkidu. Just what every customer inevitably does, Siduri thought. Of course, they were amazing exploits this time, not your run-of-the-mill bravado. Gilgamesh flaunted the crazed energy of someone who still lives in hope, though grief over Enkidu ate away at his confidence. He still hadn't given up the idea that death was something you could root out, like Humbaba and his cedars.

"There was only one way to interrupt those stories, and it always worked. 'Impressive,' Siduri said. 'So what's with the hollow cheeks and glazed eyes?'

"Gilgamesh fell silent for a moment, taken by surprise. How was it that this woman seemed to know everything? And he began to speak of the only thing he really cared about and that he could have talked about all night: Enkidu, his dead friend.

"It was then that Siduri, with sovereign sobriety, told him what I would have to tell him again later, weaving it together with other stories: 'When the gods fashioned men, they assigned them death and kept life for themselves.' Not a word more was required. And no one could have said it better than Siduri, used as she was to standing quietly behind the bar, listening to the endless, empty monologues of her customers.

Who were always enchanted by her, by her veiled beauty, her golden cups, her silence that they mistook for interest.

"Despite what she had said, Gilgamesh asked Siduri how to find me. I was his last conceivable goal. And soon afterward, he left in a whirl. Siduri had seen him only that one night, but she seemed to know everything that I would find out about him only after many days. Seeing Siduri became a way of remembering Gilgamesh. And she felt the same way."

"After the apparition that was Gilgamesh, there was a long, interminable period in which nothing happened. If my task had been to dispel Gilgamesh's last illusions, I had certainly done the job and could now consider myself superfluous. I began to think the Anunnaki had forgotten me. I was no use to them anymore. And perhaps they were no use to me, who would never die. But I felt no relief. On the contrary, a new poison seeped into me.

"Then one day I woke and saw another man sleeping in my tent. He must be a shipwrecked sailor. That was my first thought. We began to talk. Your stories amused and distracted me. But all at once I realized that I was the one who kept telling the stories. More and more often, you held your peace. One day it occurred to me that perhaps the Anunnaki had wanted this; they had arranged it all.

"They wanted a voice to tell the stories that had happened before the Flood. And I was the only one still alive. I had been part of those stories, or they had been told to me.

"All stories happened before the Flood. After that the only stories are stories of shipwrecks. There are always a discrete

number of shipwrecks. Seven. Or three hundred. And they always finish the same way. Whereas the stories from before the Flood are linked together. I have yet to see an end of them. That's why I have gone on speaking to you. Sometimes I had the feeling I was speaking to myself. But now I know that those stories, or at least splinters of them, and always with big gaps between one and another, are alive in you, too. Like me, they have escaped death."

VII

One morning, Sindbad spoke up first, as if he couldn't help himself:

"When I opened my eyes in this room the first time and realized there was someone lying down near me, I was overcome by terror. You are the oldest of the old and the most alive of the living. But what did I know of that, then? I had met another old man once on my journeyings; again, it was after a shipwreck. And more than any monster, he had me living in fear and torment.

"He was a handsome man, wrapped from head to toe in a cloak of woven leaves. I thought he must have been shipwrecked too. He looked at me and tried to get to his feet, but couldn't. He begged me to carry him on my back so that we could go looking for fruit. The island was full of it. I picked him up and sat him on my shoulders and began to walk. There was an exact moment when I realized his legs had fastened tightly, irretrievably, around my neck. A viselike grip I couldn't loosen. No longer covered with leaves, they were bare, rough, and dark, like buffalo hooves.

"It was the first of many desperate days. I soon sensed that

nothing was going to change. I followed the old man's orders, but couldn't sleep because his legs were choking me. He simply ignored me. He emptied his bowels down my back. I was caked in his excrement. He would kick me in the stomach when he wanted me to move. I had begun to think that life would go on like this until my dying breath. As though that awful burden had become part of my body.

"Then one day it was over. I had managed, with enormous effort, to get some juice to ferment in the shell of a gourd. I tasted it and felt it work on me, relaxing me. The old man was curious. He wanted to try the strange liquid himself. After some time I felt the grip of his legs, that iron collar that suffocated me all day long, slackening. The old man sank into drunkenness.

"As soon as I had freed myself, I started running and didn't look back. I didn't want to see the old man ever again. As on other occasions, I had the luck to find a ship that took me on board. I tried to explain what had happened to me. It was hard but I couldn't help myself. Strangely, they barely bothered to listen, as if I were telling an old story everyone knew. I asked why. One of the sailors said: 'That must have been the Old Man of the Sea. You were lucky. Those who meet him don't usually come back to tell the tale.' From time to time people have asked me: what is drunkenness for? Now I know: to free yourself from the grip of the Old Man of the Sea. But first you have to meet him."

Utnapishtim sat in silence. Suddenly he said:

"Sindbad, you have seen many seas and could spend a long time talking about their differences. But now that you have

come here, you must discover the one sea you haven't seen: the Apsu, boundless fresh water lying beneath the entire surface of the world and encircling it. Here in Dilmun it's easy to get down to those waters. They are the final surprise, the final wonder that awaits you, after all the shipwrecks you've survived.

"You mustn't imagine that the waters of the Apsu are an ocean, like others you have known. Even before the Anunnaki appeared, before names were announced, before the destinies were fixed, the Apsu was already there. And to understand the gods, the names, the destinies, you have to go through the Apsu. Being close to the Apsu was the supreme privilege Ea granted me, the way you keep a plant constantly moist. Otherwise, the Anunnaki think of me as a guard at his post. Sometimes they let me know they are expecting news. Which for the most part doesn't arrive.

"From the early days of the Flood right through to today, I have always lived in Ea's protecting shadow, never wearied of admiring his capacity to govern everything that is number, measure, weight. And every time I witnessed the clash of rude and deadly powers, I knew that his hand and his counsel, his cunning and his covert irony, would step in to avoid the irreparable and divert, if only for a while, the ruinous rush of events.

"The Anunnaki hankered after hymns, celebrations, praise pure and simple. Ishtar, Ninurta, Nergal, Marduk—they could never get enough. But there were few hymns to Ea. Yet those that there were addressed him as the god of supreme knowledge, in words not used for the other gods. Attributing him with the guardianship of divine powers. There was no predicament so oppressive, even for the Anunnaki, that Ea's astuteness

could not solve it. Yet Ea always stayed apart from the other gods.

"Ea's palace was quite different from the sanctuaries of Babylon and Uruk. It was built on the boundary between the Apsu and the Ocean. They called it the House of the Sea. It was made of silver and lapis lazuli, not one next to the other, but fused together. It radiated light where there was none. It sat solid on the waters, a marvel. With the lagoon all around and thick stands of bamboo. It was the only place Ea found congenial. He had lived in the heavens in the past, beside the Anunnaki, but chose to move far away. If necessary, he could pay them a visit."

"To know Ea one must go back, to a time before the names, and with the names the destinies. The first two names were Apsu and Tiamat, kindred waters. Others who had names were born after them and within them. A band of siblings began to stir and disturb. It could hardly be otherwise since they rested on the waters and their powers were still undefined. Apsu was troubled.

"A rule emerged: if a divine being generates other beings, he will soon be irritated by their commotion. Apsu wanted to exterminate those still shapeless generations. Tiamat didn't agree: 'We generated them, why destroy them so soon?' So she spoke, irritated herself.

"But there is always a wicked counselor. He was called Mummu and he told Apsu that if he didn't kill off those children he would never get any rest. Mummu knew that all Apsu wanted was to rest through the day and sleep through the night. Perhaps Apsu's sleep was more adventurous than any other's

wakefulness. And there is always someone who snoops and tells tales. The turbulent gods got wind and were scared. All at once they crouched down and kept quiet. Only Ea stepped up. This was the moment that changed everything. From then on, people began to say that Ea understood everything.

"There was no question of attacking Apsu like any ordinary adversary, because Apsu was everywhere. Ea chose another way. Instead of winding him up, he gave him a potion that helped him sleep, which is what Apsu wanted. Mummu tried it too, and sank into a torpor. Deftly, silently, Ea set about stripping Apsu, one by one, of his talismans: his crown, the band around his forehead, the cloak of splendor he wrapped himself in. Then he killed his sleeping father.

"He hadn't finished. He took hold of Mummu, tied him up, and put a ring through his nose. Then looked around. Ea knew that Apsu wasn't just a god and a father of gods. Apsu was also a place. So Ea decided to make this place his home. Here he would build his watery palace. Here he would welcome his spouse, Damkina, into the bridal chamber. And here one day she would give birth to Marduk, who was celebrated as first-born of the Apsu."

"When Tiamat decided to avenge the death of Apsu, Ea didn't say a word. He shut himself up in a room in silence. Would he have to kill his mother, too? Meanwhile, frightening sounds were heard from the distant world. Tiamat was organizing the attack. She had generated eleven monsters, filling them with poison instead of blood. They included the Hydra, the Scorpion Man, the Fish Man, the Powerful Bull, and they would serve

as her bodyguards. She also gave them a captain, Kingu. She chose him as her lover and seated him on a throne. She had no plans to be a widow. And at once Tiamat fixed the Tablet of Destinies to Kingu's chest.

"Waiting for the attack, the Anunnaki were terrified. The primordial Anshar accused Ea of having caused a disaster. But by this time Ea had found his voice again, and his skill in using it. He said he had done right by everyone in killing Apsu. They would never have got another chance. Anshar calmed down and ordered Ea to use his sorcery to stop Tiamat. In a show of obedience, Ea set off. But then stopped. From far away he could already hear the roar of Tiamat and her eleven monsters. He knew they would overwhelm him. He went back to Anshar and told him his sorcery wasn't enough.

"In the end, it was Marduk who killed Tiamat. And only after listening, in a locked room, to his father's advice. Ea would never kill with his own hands again. Even when, at his instigation, Kingu was killed, Ea didn't touch him until the blood was already streaming down his torn breast. That was the blood he then used to make men. But right up to that moment, he had only watched."

"This was the sequence of events. Ea carried out the first killing. He struck down his father, a creature without limits, but for a moment vulnerable. An act to abhor or to celebrate forever. Which in actual fact was only rarely remembered. While nothing would equal the noisy celebrations for Marduk, Ea's son, when he killed Tiamat, bereft of Apsu. From that point

on, everyone spoke of Apsu as if he had always been a place, not a god at all. A place that belonged entirely to Ea. The other gods would go down there only as visitors. This in itself suggested the difference and distance between them and Ea."

"After killing his father, Apsu, Ea could have gone back to the heaven of the Anunnaki. Instead he stayed put. Apsu's body became a boundless, liquid place where Ea reigned with his consort, Damkina. If the Anunnaki called a counsel, Ea had to set out from the Apsu to join them. Otherwise he kept away. He was a solitary, remote god. It's a trait he somehow passed on to me.

"Ea had no need to call himself a king. But he was the only one who could legitimize or dethrone kings. At first the *mes* and the Tablet of Destinies were immersed in the Apsu together with Tiamat. And they would occasionally go back there. Without the *mes* and the Tablet of Destinies, no one could claim sovereignty."

"Ea killed his father, Apsu, but he stepped back when the other gods asked him to kill his mother, Tiamat. Tiamat was vaster than any other being in the world. How could one even think of overcoming her? Only the youngest of his sons, Marduk, might do it. So Ea thought. And immediately set about persuading him, refusing to give up. He told Marduk: 'I killed my father, Apsu. Now it's up to you, my son, to kill Tiamat.' He offered precious advice as to how Marduk should go about it.

If he succeeded, great honors and privileges awaited him, his father added. In everyone's mind, Ea was established as the first and wisest of counselors, but he was also the first to have killed.

"When the young god Marduk decided to march against Tiamat, there was a moment that would later be celebrated and represented, etched in stone any number of times before being forgotten. He climbed on his chariot, which was called Invincible Tempest. He had harnessed four horses to it, ready to attack. And he wasn't alone. Beside him he had the god Amuru, the charioteer. Marduk's weapons were the bow and the net. And the seven winds that were to wreak havoc on Tiamat. The gods had told him: 'Go and cut Tiamat's throat, and may the winds bring us her blood like good news.' The same gods who hadn't dared attack Tiamat had chosen Marduk as their champion, to defend them. And at first they stuck by his side.

"The chariot advanced and a company of gods marched with him. Ten up front. Fifteen right behind. There were gods we don't know much about. And there were some of the most glorious gods: Ea and Damkina, Marduk's parents, and Ninurta, Mullissu, and Beletili, who was the mother of other gods.

"Yet all of a sudden, Marduk found himself facing Tiamat alone. At first he spoke to her. He even had the gall to scold her for having allowed Kingu, a traitor god, to take Apsu's place in her bed. Tiamat mumbled, as witches will. Deadly spells. And gradually her fury swelled. The two clashed. Marduk cast his net. When Tiamat opened her immense mouth, Marduk thrust in one of his evil winds, to stop it closing. At the same time, he loosed an arrow in Tiamat's belly. And flung himself on the wound, to open the gash. Thus Tiamat was slain. The gods who had taken Tiamat's side had disappeared, terrified. All that re-

mained was to get hold of the Tablet of Destinies, which Tiamat had given to Kingu for safekeeping. Marduk hunted him down, grabbed the Tablet, placed his seal on it, and fixed it on his chest.

"For a while, he stood motionless, in silence. Now the world had to clothe itself in those two divine corpses. Marduk wanted marvels from them. Skillfully, like a fishmonger at the market, he cut Tiamat's body in half. What to do with it? Deck out the world. Then he measured Apsu's body, which was still lying there, and used it to make Esharra, the heavenly sanctuary, a copy of which would later be built on earth. He began to arrange the constellations on the dark canvas of the sky. And decided what order they should move in: he split up time into the days of the year. Tiamat's liver he placed at the Zenith. And caused the Tigris and the Euphrates to spring from her eyes.

"The Anunnaki weren't satisfied. They were happy to have been freed from Tiamat's oppression and one by one they kissed Marduk's feet, but they still had another favor to ask of him. They wanted a place where they could rest at night when they were down on earth. 'Build Babylon!' said Marduk. 'Mold the bricks, raise up the sanctuaries!' The Anunnaki set to work. For two years, like apprentice bricklayers, they fashioned clay into bricks. At last they found themselves gazing on the Esagil, the Eminent House, a city within the city."

"Apsu was killed by his son Ea. Then Tiamat by Ea's son Marduk. The world continued to be made up of their measureless bodies, from the fresh subterranean waters to the vault of the heavens, Tiamat's back, which Ea neatly flattened out and studded with stars.

"The measureless remains of the two primordial gods stretched out in every direction. Still whole, Apsu became Ea's home. Tiamat was cut into pieces. One piece was attached to the heavens. Another was wrapped around the world's axis. The lower part of her body formed the mountains and the springs of the Tigris and the Euphrates.

"Marduk stabilized the cosmos once and for all. He used Tiamat's belly as a wedge to keep the earth, the heavens, and the Apsu separate and stable. Until then they had been indistinct from one another, something the Anunnaki found intolerable. So they let Marduk concentrate their powers in himself."

"Babylon was Marduk's invention. Obeying his orders, the Anunnaki worked at it till the Esagil was stark against the sky. They called it the palace of the pleasure of the gods of the heavens, the house that radiates splendor, the house with the high roof, the house that creates all the gods, the house that does all and loves the truth, bond of the heavens. Around the Esagil were built forty-three sanctuaries of the Great Gods. While the Anunnaki dwelled in the heavens and occasionally came down to their temples, Marduk wanted just one residence, in Babylon's Esagil. And Marduk claimed to contain all the gods in himself. He had transformed them into so many epithets. Thus with Marduk the gods found themselves all living together on earth. It was a huge change, and one that was bound to have consequences.

"Babylon was often called Eridu. The last of the great cities clothed itself in the name of the first. It was a prophetic allusion to the fact that Babylon would put a seal on time. A New Bab-

ylon would never arise, because the Anunnaki had already melted away. The name Esagil was there in each phase of each epoch. In the beginning, Ea had built his temple in the Apsu. Then he had made a copy of it in his city, in Eridu, and called it the Esagil. Finally, Marduk founded a new city, Babylon, that had at its center an Esagil built on Tiamat's body. One passed from father to son and from the Apsu to Tiamat. The epochs went by and the same names came around. Until the circle closed."

"Like others Marduk would end up proposing the creation of men. The Anunnaki were stuck with the same old conundrum: how to be rid of all their burdens. And the only way to keep them happy was to make beings of flesh and blood who could do the hard work for them. And the blood had to be a god's blood. But which god? Ea was ready with his advice: they should kill the god who had incited Tiamat to fight the Anunnaki: Kingu, her temporary lover. With Ea watching, Marduk and the other gods caught him, tied him up, and held him still. Then they cut open his chest, so that the blood needed to make men could gush out."

Sindbad looked at Utnapishtim, perplexed:

"But wasn't the story rather different?" he said.

"With the Anunnaki certain things can happen more than once," Utnapishtim told him, and went on:

"Marduk, the new arrival among the gods, hadn't come merely to free them from the oppression of Tiamat. He had come to humiliate them. He had tied up Anshar, the primordial god, Anu's father, and reduced Enlil to dust and water. He even forced Anu off his heavenly throne, obliging him to hide

among the ranks of the Anunnaki. And he tore his heart from his chest. He covered it with Dumuzi's blood, which streamed down into the Apsu. Even Ea, his father, was mistreated; Marduk tossed him into the Apsu, which was his home. It was a terrible offense. And no one had ever dared offend Ea before."

"Marduk had fifty names that celebrated him in every way. The Tablet of Destinies, however, was never mentioned. Yet after killing Tiamat, the first thing Marduk had done was hand the Tablet over to Anu. Was this an act of homage to the god of heaven? Who can say? Marduk himself would destroy Uruk, the city of Anu, and Nippur too, the city of Enlil. The passage from one divine regime to another is always violent and cruel. Marduk guaranteed the gods their security even as he overthrew them, first and foremost Enlil."

"Marduk wasn't always victorious. And the insults, harassment, and anxieties he had inflicted on the Anunnaki did not go unpunished. But what they found absolutely unacceptable was that Marduk should presume to assimilate the powers into his fifty names. He might as well have been telling the Anunnaki they had suddenly become superfluous.

"As a result, something happened that people did not talk about willingly. The first gods, the fathers, took their revenge. They laid siege to this son who claimed to have saved them. And they did it in the most sacred of places, the Esagil, the temple in Babylon that Marduk had made his home.

"As though sensing what was to happen, Nabu made haste from Borsippa to visit his father. But Marduk was already imprisoned. Led by Anshar, who was angrier than all of them, the first gods had entered the Esagil and set about plundering it. Nothing precious would escape them. Marduk had taken refuge in one of the temple's cells and barred the door. The gods burst through, attacked Marduk, and tied him up.

"'You'll be judged as a criminal, not a god,' they told him. Outside, the crowd was rioting. Many bore grudges against this most recent god. Marduk was dragged down to the riverbank, as was the custom for the worst offenders. They had torn off his ceremonial robes and his body bore witness to the beatings he had taken. Only Ishtar said she felt sorry for him and for Nabu. But she couldn't stop the gods. They brought a common criminal to stand beside Marduk. This man, too, was to be judged. They cut off his head and hung it from Ishtar's neck. While judgment was passed on Marduk, a priest with a piercing voice read the beginning of the poem about the origins that was usually read in its entirety at the festival to inaugurate the year. Rather than to the glory of Marduk, this time the poem was dedicated to the glory of Anshar. No one knows for sure what happened to Marduk then. He disappeared from Babylon and his statue with him. Years later, when he reappeared, some said it had all happened because the statue needed restoring."

"Marduk had lost interest in ruling. He had given the other gods peace and quiet in return for their powers. No one complained save Nergal, the most inaccessible of gods, on his throne

in the Underworld. When Nergal chose to be called Erra, he became fire and plague, darting across the earth and bringing devastation. Nothing could stop him. But this wasn't enough. Erra was full of rancor. He felt his name wasn't properly recognized. He watched Marduk idle on his throne, blank and grim, even though no one was opposing him. The time had come to show him that he, Erra, was still a real, untamed power.

"When he sensed Erra was close by, Marduk roused himself from his torpor. And decided to remind the other of his exploits. He didn't even mention the most famous, the killing of Tiamat. Instead, with some effrontery, he spoke of having decreed the Flood, which wasn't true. Then he recalled things he'd done that had changed the world and that people rarely mentioned. He had caused the Apkallu to disappear into the Apsu. They must never again be seen on earth. Knowledge would become invisible. Then he reminded Nergal of his most mysterious exploit: he had moved the tree *mesu*, that was called *flesh of the gods*, and had never revealed where he had put it. That tree was the emblem of the King of the World. In the beginning, it had stretched its roots for hundreds of miles in the Apsu and its crown rose to Anu's heaven. Moving that tree had changed life forever. And no one would ever be able to take it back to where it had once been. Marduk was suggesting that even if Erra were to lay the entire world to waste, nothing essential would be changed. Whatever he did it wouldn't have any effect on the *flesh of the gods*. As for men, there would always be a *remnant*, ready to pick up the same life and perform the same ceremonies all over again.

"Erra didn't let this stop him. He wanted to show the gods that the rites were no use at all if he was causing havoc. He

wouldn't just kill men himself, they would kill one another. Circling like a hawk that draws nearer and nearer, Erra destroyed Sippar, the primordial city that even the Flood had spared. Then he destroyed Uruk, city of prostitutes and hierodules, dear to Ishtar and Anu. Finally, he came to Babylon, ready for the massacre. Then Marduk felt a pang in his heart and spoke words he had never spoken before. He said he had planted Babylon like a lush orchard but had never tasted its fruits. He said he had taken Babylon into his hands as he had taken up the Tablet of Destinies and he would not surrender it to anyone.

"But it was the counselor Ishum who prevented the calamity, interrupted it rather, as if it were something that had already happened. He told Erra he had already achieved all his goals. He had struck down the just and the unjust; he had killed girls in their beds and priests as they prepared offerings; he had pulled down sanctuaries. Never again would the gods look down on him. And so it was. The Igigi and the Anunnaki stared at him, daunted, petrified. Erra insisted he could devastate everything whenever he liked. If he hadn't finished the job, it was only because the wise counselor, Ishum, had persuaded him to leave a *remnant*. The gods would have to make do with it. And this remnant included Babylon. But one day, Babylon, too, would be destroyed and the remnant would shift elsewhere."

"Some of these stories reached me in the form of riddles. And sometimes those riddles emerged in certain ceremonies. I see the king advancing on a chariot toward the temple of Enmesharra, the defeated god. Enmesharra's corpse was lying on the chariot. Beside the king there was a priest and he was

singing. The king represented Ninurta and in his hand he held the tongues of Anzu.

"I have thought a great deal about these stories without managing to reconstruct them in every part. One thing I am sure of, though: after Marduk, all other gods ceased to appear, as if they had become extinct, or killed one another off. And living without gods, people found, was not only acceptable, but easy."

VIII

The emptiness stretched away in all directions. A dense, gleaming, unbounded emptiness. Of bamboo, palms, thorns, ditches, sand. This was Dilmun. But you never felt sure it would still be there, if once you closed your eyes.

"That must be because it is so near to the Apsu," said Utna-pishtim, sensing the question Sindbad was about to ask. And he went on:

"There are no temples here in Dilmun, and no houses. There are no inhabitants. No crops are sown. What grows grows. The island is rough and flat, with occasional dunes. Which look like burial mounds, tombs, of whom I couldn't say. Here in Dilmun the only thing that happens, now and then, is that the wind shifts.

"In the times when I was king, nothing was so small as to have no importance. And this weighed on us. It was a big part of the burden the Anunnaki had loaded on us. Often we found ourselves thinking we would have gladly let be. But we couldn't. Chance didn't exist. Even the animals offered as sacrifices had their destinies etched into their hides.

"Then the Anunnaki withdrew. When they do reappear, very likely no one notices. For some they have become an object of curiosity. Chance, on the other hand, is now dominant, it is worshipped. And is no less inflexible. It does no one any favors. This is all that I have been given to see."

"I'm telling these stories of the Anunnaki as if Ea had instructed me: 'You will live and tell our stories.' But Ea never said that. Ea never explained anything. He governed by allusion. Perhaps that's why he chose me: I was good at guessing allusions.

"Ea even granted me a glimpse of the Underworld. They called it the Great City. Many Anunnaki lived there, gods who would never again climb the ladder to heaven. Everything converged on the point where the sovereign sat: Ereshkigal. Beside her, Nergal. Both of them silent, motionless. But if Nergal did show himself on earth, devastation followed in his path. He was greedy for the dead.

"Some thought the two had reigned as a couple from the beginning. But their story was very different. Travel between the Anunnaki in heaven and the Underworld was impracticable. Ereshkigal couldn't go to the banquets in heaven, and the Anunnaki in heaven couldn't go down to the Underworld to visit her. So they sent gifts and paid homage to each other. On one occasion, Nergal refused to stand up to greet a minister from Ereshkigal. This was an insult that could have upset the order of things forever. Ea advised Nergal to make amends by going down to Ereshkigal, well protected by a company of

deathly powers and careful not to fall into certain traps. One of
which was Ereshkigal's beauty. Ea knew that the queen would
use the excuse of taking a bath to undress before Nergal. Who,
however, must resist.

"What happened was quite different. Ereshkigal was shoved
off her throne and knocked to the ground; then Nergal was
about to cut off her head when the queen invited him to be-
come her spouse. For six days and six nights they coupled with-
out cease. Then Nergal decided to return to heaven. Ereshkigal
despaired. She said she had never played and danced as a little
girl, knew none of earth's pleasures. The only pleasure she had
had was from Nergal. If she couldn't go on having it, she threat-
ened to have the dead rise up and devour the living.

"When the Anunnaki saw Nergal back among them again,
they were anxious. They knew that order had not been restored;
on the contrary, it had been even more deeply disturbed. Ea
proposed to Nergal that he go back down to the Underworld.
And Nergal obeyed. He reappeared before Ereshkigal, but this
time he smiled, slipped the shawl from her neck, and started
coupling with her again. From that day on the two were never
apart."

"More than Babylon or Eridu, it was the Underworld that
was the Great City. Walking through it, one came across one
palace after another. Some said: 'This is Nergal's palace, this is
Ereshkigal's.' But there were others, too, palaces of the minor
gods, Hushbisha, Dimpimeku, Ninazimue. There were temples,
too, and towers. Darkness was constant, except when Utu, the

Sun, made a brief visit to pass judgment. The inhabitants wandered in the dust, dressed in feathers down to their feet, like birds that cannot fly. They ate clay."

Now it was Sindbad who spoke:

"I, too, once saw a Great City thronged with the dead. I may also have seen its queen. I was part of Emir Musa's retinue. One among many. We were crossing the desert, a colorful caravan. All of a sudden, along the horizon, an unbroken black line appeared. Everyone saw it. The walls of the City of Brass, forged in a single mold. The nearer we came, the more compact the dark line became. We were waiting to make out the city gates. There were twenty-five, but you couldn't see any sign of them on the surface. We walked right around the immense city several times, trying to find a way in. In the end, we made long ladders to climb over. The first to try were the baggage carriers. They climbed up and, one after another, stood motionless for a few seconds, never very long, gazing into the city. Then they burst into exasperated laughter and, with that grating sound still hanging in the air, they plunged down below. It happened to every single one, without exception, as though in a ceremony.

"We were horrified, but no one wanted to give up. Walking along the walls, we found a statue in a niche, the statue of a horseman with one hand outstretched. On the hand there was a written sign showing which point of the statue to press to open a gate in the walls. Soon enough we found the broken bodies of our companions. We pressed on into the city.

"I have never seen such perfect order. Everything was just so, everything glittered. All the shops were open. Metals, cloths,

carpets, and jewels were on display. The metals shone. We soon saw the guardians of the place. They were lying on beds of silk or seated on high chairs: dead, unblemished. The only sounds came from the birds darting over the roofs. Plants and trees were in bloom. Inside every shop, deep in the half-light, you could just see the shopkeeper, alert, carefully dressed, fossilized. The streets were empty.

"Finally, we found ourselves outside an immense palace. We crossed four pavilions, one inside another, full of precious things. The soldiers watching over them and the guards at the door had leather for skin. Hall after hall drew us on to a last room clad in marble and ivory. A woman gleaming like the moon lay stretched on a big bed, protected by two warriors, who looked like statues. Her eyes had been replaced with mercury, like a doll's. It was impossible to escape their gaze, which was in constant movement. One of Emir Musa's squires made to grab a dazzling jewel from the woman. One of the warriors was an automaton. He lifted his saber and cut off the man's head."

IX

"Shortly before the Flood, I was king of Shuruppak. It wasn't the center of the world, but it wasn't far off. My grandfather Ubartutu had founded the dynasty. Of my father it was said that he was a wise man of fine words. Of me, people said only that I would have a long life. My father put together a collection of sayings, some in the form of proverbs, and dedicated it to me. For the most part, they offered advice on how to behave toward other men. Only rarely did they touch on the gods. But the gods were implied. I was able to observe those rules only for a very brief part of my life, tiny in proportion to the years I've spent alone here in Dilmun. But I still remember them. Sometimes they make me smile; they are so distant now, incomprehensible almost. Other times they seem perfect, radiant. They weren't rules for men who must govern. But for anyone.

"Of the words people used when I was king of Shuruppak, many have gone now, disappeared. Most of them were buried under the sand, suffocated while waiting for someone who would let them breathe again. Then in some cases, they were

substituted, high-handedly, as if they had just been invented. Only one of those words is still omnipresent, though used each time in different ways. Nevertheless, it has remained on everyone's lips, from the washerwoman to the king. The word *destiny*. If it weren't for that word, you wouldn't be here today."

"Anzu was an eagle with a lion's head, his body clad in chain mail. When he wasn't flying, he stood on his claws like a powerful man. It was Ea who suggested to Enlil that they could use Anzu as guardian of the threshold, to protect the hall where Enlil would immerse himself in the sacred water. Was it treacherous advice? Some doubt remains, as with so much of what Ea did.

"Anzu was the only witness when Enlil undressed, removed his crown, the band around his forehead, the cloak of sovereignty. And last of all the Tablet of Destinies, which he always kept hanging from his chest. While Enlil was naked, immersed in the water, Anzu snatched the Tablet and flew off toward a mountain that even the Anunnaki could not climb.

"Everyone was shocked. They knew their lives couldn't go on without that clay tablet, though it hardly differed, to look at, from so many others used in earthly palaces to etch administrative documents, omens, and grocery lists. They also knew, and soon got confirmation, that none of them had the courage to follow Anzu and fight him.

"Once again, it was Ea who took control. He suggested they turn to Mami, queen of all the Anunnaki, who got involved only in very rare instances. And Mami pointed to her son Ninurta as the one to fight Anzu.

"It was a duel like no other. And even here, Ea gave the decisive advice that allowed Ninurta to clip Anzu's wings. In the end, the Tablet of Destinies was recovered. But for a long time Ninurta was reluctant to return it to his father, Enlil. Only when he was promised a long list of honors and privileges did he finally, grudgingly, hand it back. The Anunnaki could feel safe again. Enlil rediscovered his shine."

"The duel was all but over. Anzu had folded his wings. His claws opened and he let go his grip on the Tablet. Which fell down all the way to the Apsu, drawn to its place of origin. Aching and bruised, Ninurta had to go down there and persuade Ea to let him have the Tablet. It was a last, arduous ordeal. Only then could Ninurta climb back up to the Anunnaki and hand over the Tablet to Enlil. And the world emerged from the paralysis that had left it stiff and arid.

"The Anunnaki were never self-sufficient, though many imagined otherwise. They needed an object in which everything that was and was becoming the world could concentrate: the Tablet of Destinies. Now they had it back in their care again, though they were bound to remember that in the beginning the Tablet had lain in the Apsu and in Tiamat, that immense enemy power.

"When Marduk reappeared, after his victory over Tiamat, the first thing he did was to give the Tablet to Anu, just as Ninurta returned it to Enlil. Gestures of homage, but also of liberation."

"Like an army forever changing formation, the Anunnaki were everywhere, among the stars, on the earth, in the Underworld. In the beginning, as I was told, there were thirty-three of Enlil's gods around the Pole, fifteen of Ea's gods near the Equator, and twenty-three of Anu's in the areas between. A celestial equilibrium. Finally, Marduk decided to impose some order. As the newly crowned king of the gods, this was his job. It was the first census of all time. It turned out there were three hundred gods of heaven, guarding Anu's decrees. Another three hundred gods resided in the Underworld. Then there were the fifty Great Gods and the seven gods of fate, the Sebittu.

"The most elusive to my mind were always the gods of fate. Anu had his celestial decrees that were to be protected. But clearly there were other decrees that came neither from the Anunnaki nor the Igigi, but from these gods who were simply called the Seven. I've always wondered if they weren't the most powerful of all. Yet today, as then, I can't say for certain.

"The Tablet of Destinies had emerged from the Apsu. And no one knew the Apsu better than Ea, who had killed Apsu and who lived there. The god who had the Tablet of Destinies fixed on his breast believed he held supreme power. And if someone took it away from him, as when Anzu took it from Enlil, not only would his power fade, but his splendor, too. This was what those watchful guardians the gods forever feared."

"What was written on the Tablet of Destinies? Order. So long as the Anunnaki had control of the Tablet, they knew how to celebrate the rites and implement the law. If they didn't have it, things fell apart. But there was one detail the Anunnaki

always glossed over. When the Tablet of Destinies emerged from the Apsu and from Tiamat, it was already written on, in part. And order was written on that part, too. An order that included all calamities and all evils. Obeying the Tablet of Destinies, one was bound to accept this part, which the Anunnaki had not written.

"I knew very well that nothing had the Anunnaki panicking in their heaven so much as losing control of the Tablet of Destinies. Though this was always something external to them, a talisman to fix on your breast. Hence something that you might lose from one moment to the next. And when that happened even the greatest of the Anunnaki were plunged into a state of unknowing. I often wondered if this wasn't what happened when the bright shapes of the Anunnaki began to lose their shine, as if a fog had drifted over them, the marshland fog at the confluence of the rivers, not far from where I am now."

"The Anunnaki were not themselves order. Nor had they formulated order. The Anunnaki had appropriated order, killing its guardians, Apsu and Tiamat, then using their bodies to make the substance of the world. Tiamat clad the stars, the vault of the firmament, and the rugged surface of the earth. The Apsu was a liquid ring, a river that flowed in heaven in the Milky Way, constantly gushing from Ea's shoulders.

"Gilgamesh came to me still trusting in the power of the Anunnaki, knowing he was related to them, since two parts in three of him were divine. And I was given the unhappy task of disabusing him, recounting the mystery of the gods before the Flood. Throughout his life Gilgamesh had paid no mind to the

Tablet of Destinies, as if it were something he could replace. And now he was bound to acknowledge that this couldn't be done. Even the plant of youth that he received, as a farewell gift, not from me but from the woman beside me, was not what he was hoping for. He sought life without end, which the Anunnaki had kept for themselves. And in fact, a shrewd and watchful snake stole the magic plant from him."

"The Anunnaki didn't ask whether something was right or wrong. They asked whether or not it belonged to order. And order did not spring from any law, but from the composition of a certain number of elements, the *mes*. Of which all were required. Even the most terrible *mes*, which Ishtar rode upon. Even the panther, which drew divine powers from the Apsu.

"The earth needed a bond, a rope, tying it to heaven. Where it was fastened in Ursa Major. Should that rope snap or come untied, everything would swing loose and disintegrate in chance. That was their one enemy. Which they were careful never to name.

"The Tablet of Destinies concentrated in the smallest possible horizontal space the axis that traversed the heavens. Around that axis, keeping it strong, curled Tiamat's tail. Nothing else was required to have order rule the world. But it was always a precarious order. The celestial bond might fade away, the Tablet of Destinies might be stolen, or fall back into the Apsu. Every year, to have the year begin, the Anunnaki had to meet in counsel and renew what was written on the Tablet of Destinies, which had to remain intact.

"Nowhere else in the world, some claimed, would you find

another small object like the Tablet of Destinies. Nor were the eyes of our statues—enormous, wide-open eyes, set in pools of black—to be found elsewhere. No one worshipped talismans, spells, omens as we did. We lived in terror of everything that happens by chance. A few signs etched on a clay tablet went some way to keeping things in check. So we shut ourselves up in the four sides of that Tablet as though in a cosmic cage, something so powerful as to elude even the Anunnaki. Who watched grimly over it, knowing that its decrees couldn't be carved in stone or reproduced on innumerable other tablets. The Tablet of Destinies was the only one forever steeped in the waters of the Apsu."

"When Ea was celebrated, it was said that he *fixed the destinies*. The same was also occasionally said of Ishtar, Anu, Enlil, and Marduk. It wasn't altogether true. The Tablet of Destinies was fixed before them, when it belonged to Tiamat. But even this wasn't altogether true, because something was always being added to the Tablet. Why else were there ceremonies at the beginning of each year? Why else did they shut themselves up in the Esagil, in a cell called the *chamber of destinies*? But it is also true that none of the Anunnaki lived in the Apsu, aside from Ea. And in the beginning, the Apsu and Tiamat were not distinct from each other. Ea lived closer than anyone else to the place whence the destinies had emerged.

"There was a chamber of destinies in other temples, too, in Nippur, Borsippa, and Uruk. But which was the first, the model for all the others? Ea had just killed his father, Apsu. He had the counselor Mummu tied up with a ring through his nose. But

he did not hurry up to the Anunnaki in triumph to celebrate his victory, as his son Marduk would when he killed Tiamat. On the contrary, Ea withdrew quietly into a chamber, which was to be the chamber of destinies, the hall of interwoven orders. His spouse, Damkina, came down to him there in her splendor. And there Marduk was conceived. It was the place that governed everything that happens, and it was also a bridal chamber."

"What was life like for the Anunnaki before they took possession of the Tablet of Destinies? They did not control order. Rather, order preceded them, dominated them. They were gods, but not altogether sovereign.

"To show their unease they disturbed Apsu's sleep. Finding their noise unbearable, he decided to wipe them out. Tiamat was hard put to dissuade him. Many generations would pass from then until the day when Enlil told the Anunnaki that he couldn't sleep for the noise men were making. They would have to be wiped out. The gods decided on the Flood.

"Thanks to Ea's advice, men survived. They founded an empire. The emperor sometimes found his sleep disturbed by the noisy crowds outside his palace doors. So he had his soldiers intervene with the order to kill anyone they came across, as if they were out hunting. So time passed. There was always someone, *someone beneath, someone outside*, who disturbed a sovereign's sleep. No sovereign ever slept soundly.

"The Tablet of Destinies surpassed the power of the gods. And the gods wanted nothing more than to equate their power

to that of the Tablet of Destinies. Only then could they complete their names with the epithet *he who fixes the destinies*. Thus it was for Enlil, Anu, and Ea. But to do that they must first take possession of the tablet. And to renew and decree the single destinies the gods must unite in ceremony at the beginning of each new year. Only then could they feel secure in their power."

"The destinies were an order that somehow eluded the gods, in a way none of them wished to or knew how to explain. The only thing we know for certain is that the gods needed the destinies and the destinies did not need the gods, and even less did they need a single god. Yet it was only through the gods that one arrived at the destinies. Hence the ceremonies in the Esagil. And if the gods needed these ceremonies, men would need them all the more. Except that, at a certain point, men decided they could do without them. They stopped talking about the gods, but they never stopped talking about destiny, as you have seen yourself."

"At the time of the Flood I had been called Atrahasis, the Exceedingly Wise, because I was given the task of saving men and animals. I never believed in that name. I never felt wise. More like someone who lives not too far from the origin of knowledge, which springs from Ea. Who was not wise but knowing, which is a different thing altogether. The wise are reasonable, the knowing are inscrutable. I never even tried to fathom certain of Ea's doings. There was always something tortuous and secret

about them. Ea seemed to appreciate my not asking too many questions."

"The order that proceeds from Ea may be elusive and hidden. But it is everywhere, always. No order that man establishes, however good or bad, can hold for long. This became clear to me, once again, when I heard the story of Ahiqar.

"They called him *wise and able scribe, counselor of all Assyria.* From as early as he could remember, Ahiqar had decided to be a prudent, upright man. And so he became. He saw no higher goal in life than to be the king's counselor. A goal he duly reached.

"Everything must correspond to the established order. And so, for Ahiqar, it did, but for one shortcoming: he didn't have children. That was all it took to undermine this order. There was, however, his sister's son, Nadin. Ahiqar decided to raise the boy himself, impressing him with the principles that had ruled his own life. Not that Ahiqar had invented these principles, just tested and experimented them his life long. Practicing and accepting those principles would render Nadin as similar as possible to Ahiqar, who had chosen him.

"One day Ahiqar told the king he was feeling old and presented Nadin as his successor. The king agreed. Ahiqar could retire at last. He imagined Nadin would always act on his behalf. Instead, Nadin spoke ill of him to the king. He wanted Ahiqar dead and his memory defiled. He wanted his principles rubbed out and forgotten.

"The king believed him. He ordered that Ahiqar be killed and entrusted the task to three officers. They found him walking

in the vineyards. Ahiqar guessed at once that these three offi-
cers, appearing unannounced, had come to kill him. But Ahiqar
had once saved one of these men when he was about to be exe-
cuted. He reminded him of this and the officer decided to shelter
him in his house. But they couldn't go back to the king without
having killed someone. The officer thought of a servant of his, a
eunuch, and said to his companions: 'Kill him!' Later the king
realized he had been deceived by Nadin. Ahiqar's honor was
restored. And his story was on everyone's lips."

"Ever since I can remember, I have heard talk of the desti-
nies. I have never stopped thinking of them. One day I asked
one of the Apkallu what they are. He said: 'Necessity has no
meaning. Destiny has meaning. The destinies are an order with
meaning superimposed, point by point, step by step, on neces-
sity.' Then he slid back into the waters."

"*Destiny bites like a dog and binds like a tight gown.* Every-
one knew that saying. The Anunnaki took care to fix the des-
tinies, engaging in long ceremonies to do so. And the kings of
the earth, who imitated the Anunnaki, knew that their lives
depended on those ceremonies. No one was so innocent as
to imagine that destiny didn't bite. But they wanted destiny
to exist, and wanted it to be fixed, for each occasion, in every
place, for every king, for every year, for everybody. Better to
live bound tight by destiny than abandoned to the turbulence
of chance. That was the real, never mentioned evil, the ultimate
horror, for men as for gods."

X

One morning, as if speaking to himself, Sindbad said:

"If ever I were to go back whence I came, I wonder what I would say. When I returned from my past journeys, I would be brimming with stories, or so people said. This time it would be different. I might say I was coming back from an uninhabited island, with a mild climate, where nothing of what grows has been planted. Adding just one other thing: that there were pools of fresh water, more than in other places, and for no apparent reason."

The following morning, Utnapishtim said:

"Every time you heard the buzzing in your blood that urged you to travel, you would leave Baghdad and go down to Basra. So without knowing it you passed by the city of Gilgamesh, Uruk, buried under soil and sand. It was no more than a mound in the plain, the rough hunched back of an ass, a tell like so many others.

"In Uruk stood the Eanna. Which means 'temple of Anu.'

But that wasn't the case. The Eanna in Uruk was the temple of Inanna. This was one of her most daring exploits. She had snatched Anu's Eanna, stolen the temple of the supreme god. This was something that went against every law there was. Looking on, the Anunnaki couldn't believe their eyes.

"Just as she had boldly gone down to the Underworld, violating the realm of her sister Ereshkigal, as if it were just another country to explore, so Inanna had boldly taken from the heavens what belonged to the heavens. Worse, she had changed the god to whom it was devoted. In the Underworld she had immediately been punished. But Anu didn't react.

"It was a troubling story, something it was best not to talk about. Or to keep between a chosen few. While everyone, over the years, would tell and retell the story of Inanna going down to the Underworld. Even little children knew it.

"Uruk was called the Sheepfold, but it was a great city, the greatest of the great cities, with walls no other city could boast. Gilgamesh himself, together with the Seven Sages, the Apkallu, had designed and built them. They were the color of the prairies. The temples were built of mud bricks with strips of bamboo between them. But Inanna wasn't satisfied. She wanted stone, marble, metal. She wanted to deck herself with lapis lazuli.

"Such things, people said, could be found only in the country of Aratta, to the east, beyond seven mountain chains. A king, Enmerkar, father of Gilgamesh's father, boldly set out to cross those mountains. It was the first adventure to excite his grandson's young mind.

"More than a warrior, Enmerkar was a resourceful man. Crossing the mountains, which seemed to surround him on every side, was grueling. Enmerkar fell ill before he could join

battle with the king of Aratta. But there was more than one way for kings to fight, he thought. Bloodshed was not inevitable. Enmerkar knew that the king of Aratta was a master of riddles. Perhaps they could challenge each other with riddles. Then he could find out whether the best way forward was war or barter.

"Such was the message Enmerkar wanted to send to the king of Aratta. But it was too subtle, too unusual to be entrusted to a messenger. Very likely the messenger would make a mess of it. These people were used to delivering threats of massacres that could be announced in a few simple words.

"So Enmerkar began to etch signs on a clay tablet. They looked like seals. But Enmerkar was relying on the king of Aratta's intelligence. If he were really such a lover of riddles, he would be able to solve these mute riddles, too. Invisible to each other, concealed in the mountain forests, Enmerkar and the king of Aratta sent each other riddles and answers to riddles. They realized they had never understood anyone or been understood so well, without needing to see each other. It was the first writing, the first reading.

"Enmerkar managed to solve all the riddles the king of Aratta sent him. Then they agreed that shipments of grain, barley, and dates would be sent to Aratta. And in return Aratta would send metals, gold and silver. Lapis lazuli, too. Inanna would be satisfied at last."

"Enmerkar was Inanna and Ea's favorite. As lover to Inanna, as king to Ea. But he wasn't the only one. The king of Aratta was also a favorite of Inanna's. Both men had celebrated ceremonies

that involved the goddess getting up from their beds. Both were convinced that Inanna was on their side. Secret help was needed. When the king of Aratta challenged Enmerkar with a string of riddles, Ea, without ever appearing, suggested the answers. They could be signs etched on clay. Those tiny bars, like so many nails, would have other uses aside from resolving differences with the king of Aratta, barricaded away behind seven mountain chains. They would complicate and enhance the life of all the Black Heads. But Ea never claimed the invention as his own, as if he knew almost nothing about it. Unlike the Anunnaki, Ea never gloried in many of the things he had done."

"There were three heavens, made with different stones and different colors. Reddish gleams filtered down from the highest. The middle one was sapphire. The lower, jasper. On this heaven, Anu, Enlil, and Ea chose to trace the script of the night sky. Like silent craftsmen, absorbed by their work, they etched signs on the jasper. Which became drawings. Stars and constellations. They served as a model for Enmerkar when he etched those signs on clay.

"One day Enlil went into the goddess Nisaba's temple and laid a tablet of lapis lazuli on her knees. Then the council of the Anunnaki met. They spoke of something they called the Tablet of the Bright Heavens. It was a map of the signs that Enlil, Anu, and Ea had just etched on the jasper. From then on Nisaba would be invoked as chief scribe of heaven, goddess of the pure stylus. And an unbridgeable gap was established between Anu, Enlil, and Ea and all the other Anunnaki. These three alone had

drawn a way through heaven. And they alone each possessed a portion of the sky."

"In the beginning, men spoke one language. But understood one another too much. There were endless fallings out. Even more dangerous, though, were the moments when they reached a sudden agreement. Those were the times when they were most likely to disturb the Anunnaki. Just the noise they made had once led to the Flood. Without Ea's help they would have been wiped out. Now, having achieved an improbable unity, they were convinced they could do everything, which of course was intolerable to those looking down from above.

"Once again, life was in danger of coming to an abrupt end. Then Ea contrived another of his unresolved riddles: he multiplied the tongues of men. At first bewilderment and confusion ran riot. Then people began to split up and withdraw into different regions, well protected from one another. A dim veil came down on each of these places. But the veil could be torn open by curiosity and study. The Black Heads weren't sure whether they were more or less happy than before. They kept their eyes mainly on whatever was close to them, wanting to possess it forever. Gradually they came to forget the time when they had all spoken the same language. And the Anunnaki no longer looked on them with suspicion. Ea watched over it all in silence."

"How can you recognize a god?" Sindbad asked.

"All the gods you have encountered, or will encounter, anywhere, at the farthest edge of whatever sea, are made of the

same substance. There is a great gleaming tangle rolling over and over and constantly shedding bits of itself. And those bits are other gleaming tangles that go on rolling over and shedding other smaller bits, which again are gleaming tangles. This is the life of the gods," said Utnapishtim.

"Here is a question I have never really fathomed: whether the Anunnaki forgot about me, here in Dilmun, sometime before being forgotten themselves; or whether they left me here with a precise role in mind, the role I have in relation to you and will very likely never have again: as one who passes on their stories. If that's not the case, how can we explain why Ea, who was always such a shrewd strategist, should have taken me away from the Flood survivors to bring me here to empty, spellbound Dilmun.

"I'll confess that for a long time I tried not to think of the person who would arrive here one day, tossed up by the waves, or stepping out of a magnificent ship. But I didn't always succeed. I imagined, for example, someone who would listen to my stories attentively, skeptically. Then look at me as if I were a crazy, dangerous old man. Didn't the legends speak of a deadly Old Man of the Sea?

"Instead you arrived, Sindbad, curious, childish, clearsighted, cheeky: the perfect vessel to receive the stories entrusted to me."

"The Black Heads worshipped the Anunnaki. And the Anunnaki worshipped the Tablet of Destinies. They were devotees of

necessity, stiff, with staring eyes, thick calves, frizzy hair, cone-shaped caps, bow in hand. There was no ease or flow in their movements. Though all had their origin in Ea, who reigned over the waters. I realized this quite late, when Ea allowed me, from time to time, to wander in other lands, far beyond the two rivers, like some strange vagabond. Rather as Harun al-Rashid does in Baghdad. Had they found me out, they would have supposed I was a Chaldean con man."

"I've been here so many years and still have no answers. I've given up asking for them. Ea didn't grant me knowledge, only a life that never ends. And the sages who sometimes visit me, the Apkallu, the Holy Carp, do they have the answers? I have my doubts. Perhaps they think the world is not made to give answers."

"I know you'll be leaving soon. It's what you've always done. And I, too, shall go on doing what I've always done: staying alive."

# INDEX OF NAMES AND PLACES